Dear Readers,

I apologize for Chester's
behavior in my mouse story.
Sorry for the inconvenience.

Sincerely,
Mélanie Watt

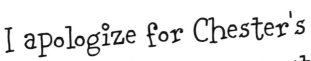
Blah! Blah! Blah!

For ~~Marcos~~, Eva, Melina and Layla

For Chester because I couldn't have made this book without him. He's the smartest, most handsome cat in the world. I wish I could be like him someday!

First paperback edition 2009

Text and illustrations © 2007 Mélanie Watt

Kids Can Press acknowledges the financial support of the Government of Ontario, through the Ontario Media Development Corporation's Ontario Book Initiative; the Ontario Arts Council; the Canada Council for the Arts; and the Government of Canada, through the BPIDP, for our publishing activity.

Published in Canada by
Kids Can Press Ltd.
29 Birch Avenue
Toronto, ON M4V 1E2

Published in the U.S. by
Kids Can Press Ltd.
2250 Military Road
Tonawanda, NY 14150

www.kidscanpress.com

The artwork in this book was rendered in pencil and watercolor and was assembled digitally.

The text is set in Carnation and Kidprint.

Kids Can Press is a CORUS™ Entertainment company

Edited by Tara Walker
Designed by Mélanie Watt
Author photo by Sophie Gagnon
Printed and bound in Singapore

The hardcover edition of this book is smyth sewn casebound.
The paperback edition of this book is limp sewn with a drawn-on cover.

CM 07 0 9 8 7 6 5
CM PA 09 0 9 8 7 6 5 4 3 2 1

LIBRARY AND ARCHIVES CANADA CATALOGUING IN PUBLICATION
Watt, Mélanie, 1975-
    Chester / written and illustrated by Mélanie Watt.

ISBN 978-1-55453-140-0 (bound)   ISBN 978-1-55453-460-9 (pbk.)

1. Cats — Juvenile fiction. I. Title.

PS8645.A884C44 2009   jC813'.6   C2008-907193-X

Chester

NOT

Written and illustrated by Mélanie Watt

KIDS CAN PRESS

Once upon a time there was a mouse.
He lived in a house in the country.

Then Mouse packed his bags and went on a trip very, very far away and we never saw him ever again!

So Chester moved in
and made a few changes
to HIS new place.

But Mouse returned home.

Oh yes, did I mention he brought back
a really big souvenir with teeth?

Back to the story ...

Once upon a time there was a mouse.

He lived in ... Chester, move out of the way!

...he lived in the country with his vegetarian dog who only ate carrots.

Then Mélanie begged Chester to write a better story. And it goes something like this ...

Once upon a time there was ME.
Chester stands for:

Charming
Handsome
Envy of Mouse
Smart
Talented
Envy of Mélanie
Really handsome

Chester lived in Chesterville,
where mice weren't allowed.
It was a beautiful day.

Until it started to rain ...

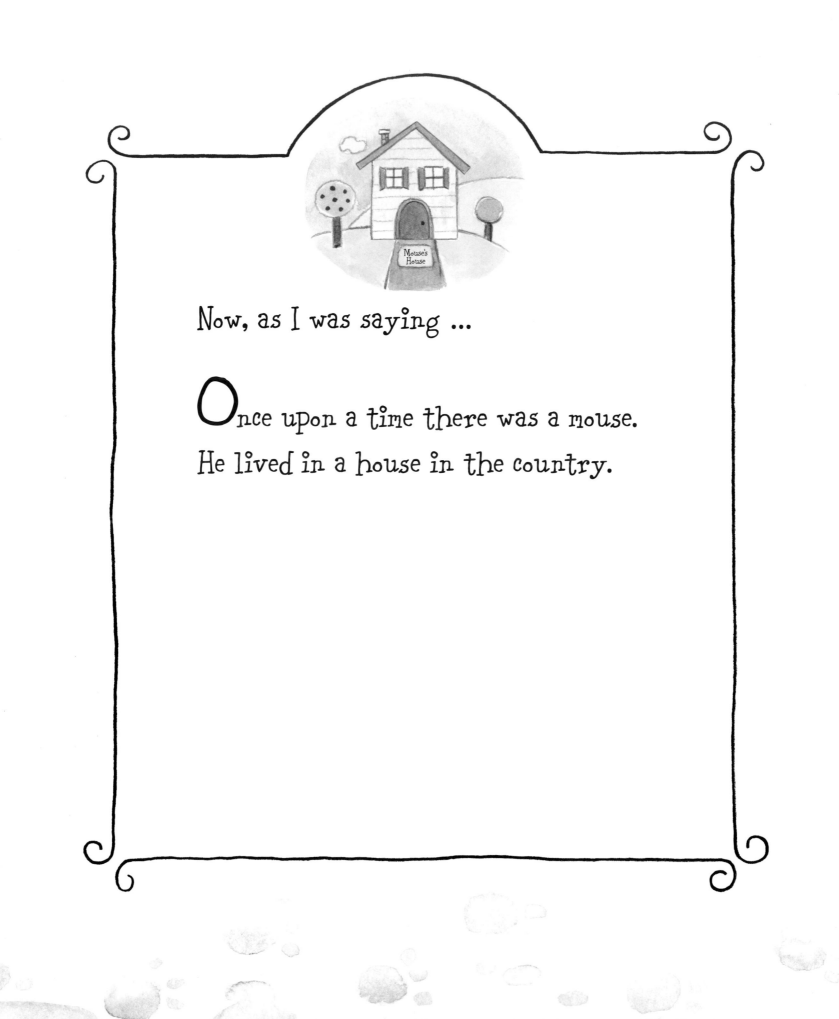

Now, as I was saying ...

Once upon a time there was a mouse.
He lived in a house in the country.

And he lived happily ever after...

Chester!
This is where I draw the line!

Nope!
I'M drawing
the line!

DO NOT cross this line!

KEEP OUT!!
(Chester's side)

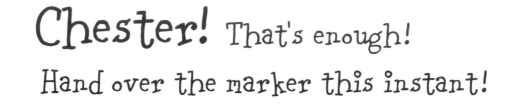

Chester! That's enough!
Hand over the marker this instant!

Chester's busy.

Chester! I'm warning you!
Hand over the marker and apologize
before I count to three!

1...

2...

3 and 4, 5, 6, 7, 8, 9, 10, 11, 12,

13, 14, 15, 16, 17, 18, 19, 20, 21...La! La! La!

All right, Chester!

You want your own story?

You want to be the star of this book?

Well, get ready. Here it is ...

FINALLY!!!

Once upon a time there was a cat named Chester.
He lived in a house in the country.

Chester was a very handsome cat.
Especially when he wore a pink ...

YOU WOULDN'T!!!

NOW it's personal ...